BOOK ANALYSIS

By Luke Hilton

Kafka on the Shore
by Haruki Murakami

BOOK ANALYSIS

Shed new light on your favorite books with

Bright
≡**Summaries**.com

www.brightsummaries.com

HARUKI MURAKAMI — 9

KAFKA ON THE SHORE — 13

SUMMARY — 17

- On a bus to Shikoku
- Nakata's not very bright
- Kafka set to music
- The entrance stone

CHARACTER STUDY — 27

- Kafka Tamura
- Satoru Nakata
- Oshima
- Hoshino
- Miss Saeki

ANALYSIS — 35

- Love and relationships
- Reality & dreams
- Fate

FURTHER REFLECTION — 45

FURTHER READING — 49

HARUKI MURAKAMI

JAPANESE WRITER

- **Born in Kyoto, Japan in 1949.**
- **Notable works:**
    - *Norwegian Wood* (1987), novel
    - *The Wind-Up Bird Chronicle* (1994), novel
    - *1Q84* (2009), novel

Haruki Murakami is a Japanese writer whose novels creatively blend Japanese and Western popular culture, with characters as passionate about anime and sushi as they are about the Beatles and pizza. His work has been translated into over 50 languages and he is one of the most successful writers in Japan's history, with an enormous international following. Perhaps indebted to the magic realist style of novel writing, Murakami's novels are often mysterious and magical, with surreal elements and aspects of narrative which are deliberately confusing or obscure.

His first novel was published in 1987 and he has published 14 more since then, as well as numerous short-story collections and essays. His works have won numerous literary prizes, and he is often a leading contender in the speculation which surrounds the Nobel Prize for Literature each year. In addition to writing novels and essays, he has translated works from English into Japanese. He is also a music fanatic and a long-distance runner, and explored the latter interest in his memoir *What I Talk About When I Talk About Running* (2007).

KAFKA ON THE SHORE

SEARCHING FOR LOST CATS

- **Genre:** novel
- **Reference edition:** Murakami, H. (2005) *Kafka on the Shore*. London: Vintage.
- **1st edition:** 2002 (Japanese), 2005 (English)
- **Themes:** identity, love, loss, friendship, music, fate, reality, gender, dreams

Kafka on the Shore is a novel concerning two related protagonists and their journeys of self-discovery. Kafka Tamura is a young boy who runs away from his father and his life in Tokyo due the parental neglect he experiences at home. His journey takes him across the country searching for meaning in his life, as well as for his missing mother and sister. As mysterious things keep happening to him and he is faced with the struggles of surviving alone as a teenager, he entrusts his life to a few key friends. In the same ward that he and his father lived in, Satoru Nakata is a well-meaning but simple-minded elderly man who, owing to an accident in wartime Japan, is not able to read or to think too deeply about anything, but can speak to cats. He uses this talent to track down the whereabouts of Tokyo's missing pets until a series of events leads him to undertake a similar journey to Kafka.

The novel, like most of Murakami's works, blends his love of surrealist storytelling with his love for food and music. The text is replete with references to jazz, classical and popular music, of both Japanese and Western origin. Similarly, in *Kafka on the Shore* Murakami is able to create a real sense of taste and smell in his descriptions of food and drink, which make the perplexing events taking place in the narrative all the more immersive.

SUMMARY

ON A BUS TO SHIKOKU

Kafka Tamura is not his real name, but like the talents and skills he learns at 15 years old, it is something he has given himself in an attempt to survive the journey he sets out on. Kafka itemises the equipment that he will take with him in his attempt to run away from his neglectful father, a famous sculptor. With his trusty back-pack he makes his way to the bus station, ready to disappear, despite being worried that he will attract attention as a 15-year-old on his own. On the bus he meets Sakura, who seems nice enough and offers him her phone number in case he wants to meet with her while he is in the city. He arrives in his new home, unsure whether he will be there long, and stays for a week in a hotel, going to the gym and to the library by day. At one point Kafka wakes up covered in blood, with no recollection as to how it got there. He calls Sakura, who helps him get cleaned up and provides a much-needed sexual release. Despite this interaction, they both wonder whether or not they might be brother and sister.

It is at the library that Kafka meets Oshima and Miss Saeki, with whom he finds employment, a place to stay, and trust. Oshima knows that Kafka is a runaway but promises to help rather than hinder, and Miss Saeki is a beautiful and enigmatic older woman who has experienced great pain and loss. Kafka goes to stay for a few days in Oshima's cabin, experiencing the majesty and terror of nature in equal measure. They confide in each other: Oshima explains that he is biologically a woman, but does not adhere to gender norms, and Kafka reveals that he believes his mother and sister ran away from him and his father when he was four years old. They discover that the night Kafka became mysteriously bloodied, his father was murdered hundreds of miles away in Tokyo. Although there was no way Kafka could have been *physically* responsible, they wonder whether he may still have been involved somehow. The police wonder this too, and they come to the library and speak to Oshima, who denies having any kind of ongoing relationship with Kafka.

NAKATA'S NOT VERY BRIGHT

Nakata can speak to cats. At the start of the novel the reader is given a number of military reports outlining a strange occurrence that happened during World War 2 in Japan, in which a series of school children (one of whom is Nakata) and their teacher go into the woods. They see something gleaming in the sky which they take for a plane and pay no attention to. Minutes later the children are all unconscious on the forest floor. Only Nakata does not wake up that day. He wakes up three weeks later unable to remember anything that had happened to him before the event, with no way of writing or reading and no knowledge of anything else. The only thing he has now that he did not have before is the ability to speak to cats. While out looking for a cat called Goma, he meets and speaks with a number of different cats, all with personalities as unique as humans. Despite his uncanny ability, he constantly tells anybody who asks that he is not very bright.

Eventually he finds that Goma is being kept, as are a number of other cats, by a man with long boots and a tall hat. What the man does with them nobody is sure, but it cannot be good. While searching for Goma he meets a large black dog who somehow transmits the message to follow him (Nakata cannot speak to dogs) and he does so, all the way to a house in an area he is not familiar with. Inside is the man who is taking the cats, who introduces himself as Johnnie Walker, an icon and marketing brand for a type of whiskey. Johnnie Walker reveals to Goma that he needs to eat cats' hearts and their souls in order to build a flute, but that he really does not want to do that. He wants to die. He tells Nakata to kill him, and says that Goma and the others will go free if he does. Although Nakata does not want to, watching Johnnie Walker maim and kill the cats in front of him brings out a mysterious anger, and he stabs Johnnie Walker through the heart. He confesses his crime to a police officer but is not believed. He also reveals to the officer that it will rain fish tomorrow. When mackerel and sardines rain down from the sky the next day, the officer realises he has messed up, but before they find the murder victim Nakata has already left Tokyo. The murder victim is a renowned sculptor and the father of a missing child, so the case becomes national news.

KAFKA SET TO MUSIC

Miss Saeki was once a successful recording artist with a song called 'Kafka on the Shore', recorded at a time just before the love of her life was murdered in a case of mistaken identity. This is a tragedy she will never recover from. Kafka Tamura, however, hears the music and loves it. He stays in the room where Miss Saeki wrote the song as a young woman and at night sees a manifestation of Miss Saeki in a ghostly form. He falls in love with the ghost, and later with the real Miss Saeki, while simultaneously believing that she may be his mother. They make love numerous times, despite their age difference. As the police step up their search operation, Oshima tells Kafka that Miss Saeki is waiting to die, and that a relationship with him is not what she should be involved in. He takes him to the cabin to lay low and to give Miss Saeki some space.

While in the woods surrounding the cabin, he comes across two World War 2 soldiers who take him to a further set of cabins and leave him there. Once there, a man approaches and reveals to Kafka's alter-ego, known as *The Boy Named*

Crow, that he makes flutes with the souls of cats. Crow takes the form of a crow and attempts to stop him by pecking his eyes out. In the cabin, Kafka's meals are being prepared by the young incarnation of Miss Saeki who appeared to him. She does not remember anything of their time together in Shikoku. When Miss Saeki arrives in the form that she existed in in Shikoku, she tells Kafka that he must leave the area, and although she will not confirm that she is his mother, she admits to having abandoned somebody and asks his forgiveness. Kafka travels back to the library, where he tells Oshima that he is going to return to Tokyo and to school.

THE ENTRANCE STONE

After Nakata leaves Tokyo, he makes his way towards Shikoku by hitchhiking with truck drivers, all of whom are kind to him and pay for his meals. Although he does not know why he is going to the next destination, he knows that it is important that he does so. He predicts when there will be thunder and lightning, and even that leeches will rain down from the sky, ending a fight taking place at a motorway rest-stop.

He meets Hoshino, a truck driver who agrees to come with him wherever he goes. Like the others, Hoshino likes Nakata and pays for his meals and for the hotels they stay in along the way. Eventually they make it to Takamatsu, where Nakata suggests they will find something called the entrance stone, although he does not say what it is an entrance for.

While out taking a walk during one of Nakata's notoriously long sleeps, Hoshino runs into Colonel Sanders of KFC fame, who promises to help Hoshino find the stone if he sleeps with a prostitute. Once he has done this, Sanders and Hoshino go to a Shinto shrine and steal the stone. Although it is heavy, Hoshino is able to take it back to Nakata in a taxi. When Nakata awakes, he tells Hoshino that in order to open the entrance the stone must be turned over. It now weighs a great deal more than it did before and it takes every ounce of Hoshino's strength to do it. Eventually he manages. Once the police have nearly caught up to Nakata for the murder of Kafka's father, Colonel Sanders puts them up in an apartment. They spend time driving around deciding what to do next. They drive past the library, and Nakata decides they should go inside, where he and Miss Saeki feel that they are connected by their histories: her inability to let go of her memories and experiences, and his inability to build memories or experiences. Shortly after their meeting, both Miss Saeki and Nakata are found dead. A cat tells Hoshino that he will have to prevent something from entering the stone, and from Nakata's body a creature emerges. He has to use all of his strength once again to flip the stone into its closed position and eventually succeeds, and he then kills the creature.

Just as Kafka leaves Shikoku full of optimism after a series of bizarre events, Hoshino leaves the hotel room and the entrance stone behind, full of hope for what his future holds.

CHARACTER STUDY

KAFKA TAMURA

Kafka is one of two protagonists in Murakami's novel, but the reader may understand his motivations more than those of Nakata due to their relatability. His problems are those that many 15-year-old boys might go through. He is obsessed with fate and finding meaning in his life, he has beliefs about his parents that seem to stem from the flimsiest of notions, and he wants nothing more than to run away where he can be free to live his life as he sees fit. Murakami invites the reader to compare Kafka with the myth of Oedipus, since Kafka's own father "cursed" him with the fate that he would sleep with his mother, as well as his sister. Perhaps this was a taunt by his father, based on Kafka's abandonment issues, but when he arrives in Shikoku he seeks to do just that. He is sexually anxious but finds an outlet with the two women that he makes himself believe are his relatives. Like most 15-year-olds, however, when Kafka makes his journey far away from his Tokyo upbringing, he does not really know what he is going to do with himself. He is guided through his naivety by Oshima, who acts like the older brother that Kafka never had.

Another guide that Kafka has throughout the novel is The Boy Named Crow. Although the true nature of Crow is never fully explained, he seems to be Kafka's inner voice of reason. He gives Kafka advice and admonishes him in his early attempts at escaping Tokyo, guiding him to what might be the right course of action. Crow is also the way in which Kafka explores the more philosophical sides of himself: "Sometimes fate is like a small sandstorm that keeps changing direction. You change direction, but the sandstorm chases you" (p. 3). In this case Crow warns Kafka that hiding from fate is pointless for him, because "this storm is you" (*ibid*).

SATORU NAKATA

The other main protagonist is Nakata, an elderly man who, in his own words, is "not too bright". As a small boy in World War 2 he was involved in a mysterious incident that involved him fainting in the woods and not regaining consciousness for three weeks. During this time his mind emptied out and left him a very friendly, but not academically capable boy. Despite his disability, Nakata is *Kafka on the Shore*'s most obviously happy character. He enjoys his life and his work talking to and finding lost cats, and before that he worked happily as a carpenter for 30 years. Although he is not able to read or write, he finds happiness in his routines, such as going to get his hair cut once a month.

People find him instantly pleasant and he is able to utilise this (although not consciously) in order to make his pilgrimage to the other side of Japan, relying on the kindness and handouts of a series of truck drivers until he finds Hoshino, his companion until the end. One possible interpretation of his ability to speak with cats is because of his ability for empathy and compassion; he speaks to cats and helps them, and converses with them because they are not judgemental towards him. Although he feels as though he was used by Johnnie Walker in order to commit murder, he rarely finds himself taken advantage of. As if by some magic he is able to avoid dangerous situations. When a gang turn their attention towards him and laugh at him, "they didn't laugh for long" (p. 208), as Nakata is unconsciously able to make it rain leeches from the sky. Towards the end of the novel he begins to realise that something is missing, that his shadow is only half as complete as other people.

OSHIMA

Oshima works diligently at the library and befriends Kafka in his time of need. He recognises the troubles that Kafka is experiencing and rather than reporting him to the police, he takes a personal risk by letting him stay in the library and in his own cabin. This personal risk is doubled when he later lies to the police about having seen Kafka. Although Oshima can be blunt, he usually does it out of friendship to either Kafka or Miss Saeki: he does not judge them for their sexual relationship (despite the enormous age difference), but only asks Kafka to end it for Miss Saeki's sake.

In addition to his caring and focused manner, Oshima is Murakami's way of exploring reality through the lens of gender identity. Although he appears to be a man and Kafka first assumes that he is male, he reveals later in the novel that he is in fact a biological woman, although he uses masculine pronouns and dates men. He describes himself as "a hopeless, damaged, homosexual gay woman" (p. 220), but the way in which he does not allow that to define his identity stops anybody from assuming that he is as damaged as he says he is.

HOSHINO

Hoshino is a regular guy, a truck driver who likes flamboyant shirts and baseball. He is the novel's *everyman* character, somebody with whom many people could identify. At first he takes only a passing interest in Nakata because he reminds him of his grandfather, but their bond builds to the point that he vows to stay with Nakata for as long as he lives. Although he might not have expected it from himself, as a self-styled slacker, his dedication to Nakata's oftentimes nonsensical mission illustrates the empathy he is capable of.

When Nakata starts to realise that he is "empty", Hoshino suffers a similar realisation. He feels bad because he believes the life he has lived has left him this way, whereas Nakata was emptied out in an accident. Of all the characters in the novel, Hoshino goes through the most personal growth. He realises that the life he was living was destroying his soul, and he finds contentment and solace in his relationship with Nakata and later his newfound love of classical music and reading.

MISS SAEKI

Miss Saeki is stuck in her past. At a young age she lost the love of her life in a horrific murder and never recovers from the pain this caused. Although she keeps busy running the library and at one time had a successful song released, she never advances beyond the emotional maturity that she had as a young woman, and is melancholic throughout the whole novel. Believing that she too has lost something innate in her, she busies herself writing books about lightning and leading an otherwise quiet life.

Kafka's appearance and sexual attraction to her open up the opportunity to rekindle her youthful love. However, it is Kafka's sighting of her

20-year-old ghost that is most revealing about her character. The fact that she has a ghost while still being alive suggests that her real death has already taken place, that what made her who she was is lost forever. She often tells Kafka and Oshima that she is not dying, but simply waiting to die. Murakami seems to suggest that she is already dead, and her body is just waiting to catch up.

ANALYSIS

LOVE AND RELATIONSHIPS

Kafka on the Shore deals with many different kinds of love. There is the love that Miss Saeki had for her murdered boyfriend Komura, which seems pure and everlasting, but ultimately is the cause of the end of her emotional life. Similarly, Kafka's sudden falling for Miss Saeki speaks to the teenage infatuations experienced by most people in their formative years. Their shared experience of love is initially positive as it gives Kafka meaning and allows Miss Saeki to rekindle her boyfriend's memory, but it is ultimately not the sort of love that these characters were meant to experience. In the last few chapters, in the surreal cabin in the woods, Kafka meets the recently departed Miss Saeki, who encourages him to go back to the real world, rather than stay with her in his perpetual youth. She tells him: "It's what *I* want. For you to be there" (p. 474). She is more like a mother to Kafka than a lover, and this final interaction between the two of them cements this type of love as being different from the one Kafka had initially imagined. She wants what is best for him. Even if she is not his real mother, she does not want him to remain in perpetual youth as she had. She wants him to go on and experience the rest that the world has to offer. Similarly, Kafka confuses romantic feelings for Sakura with the love shared between siblings, eventually realising and calling her "sister" (p. 504). As with so many aspects of the novel, the way things first appear to be can be confusing. It comes from probing within himself and with the familial love of those around him that Kafka is able to realise the truth.

The relationship between Hoshino and Nakata mirrors that of Kafka and Miss Saeki in the way it initiates as a familial affair, with Hoshino seeing the similarities between Nakata and his beloved grandfather. However, just as with Kafka, the realisation soon dawns on him that his bond with Nakata is more than just a passing resemblance to a loved one, and Nakata soon becomes an object of admiration and affection. Their friendship blossoms, perhaps because they need each other so much. Nakata relies on Hoshino for practical tasks, and Hoshino relies on Nakata for *im*practical tasks. Nakata shows him that there is a world on his doorstep he has never been able or willing to explore. His love of Nakata leads him to change things about himself that he would otherwise have ignored. He becomes stronger, more determined and more open-minded. He eventually undertakes a difficult physical task and declares that he is doing it "for Mr Nakata" (p. 487).

REALITY & DREAMS

Murakami plays enormously with ideas surrounding reality in *Kafka on the Shore*. The novel opens with an unusual event which baffles the military, the victims and scientists alike and yet, through the damage it does to Nakata, has a real and lasting effect. Joy Meads writes that "Strange things happen in *Kafka on the Shore* and it's not always immediately clear why. Like the dense, darkling imagery of Miss Saeki's song, the novel is full of images and events that resonate viscerally but resist logical explanation" (Meads, 2018). The reasoning behind events seems to be something that Murakami does not give all that much credence to. His characters simply accept that certain things happen to them and that these things are entirely possible. Kafka is covered in blood the night his father is murdered, and even though he is far from the scene of the crime, he believes that he may somehow have been responsible. Nakata can speak to cats, and when he tells people this, they very rarely do anything but nod. Things that should only happen in dreams are taken not only as acceptable, but as something tangible in their own right: "the boundary line separating the two has started to waver, to fade" (p. 290) Kafka says of the ghost and the living Miss Saeki. The fact that one defies all logic is not something that bothers him, but rather something that he strives to find a new explanation for.

Dreams and reality are recurrent themes in the novel. Murakami uses the character of Oshima to make the reader question the reality of gender. Oshima is a perfectly average-seeming person on the outside, but underneath, his reality is greatly different to that of the people around him. Murakami asks the reader to look beyond the normal surface levels and to seek what is happening in the places nobody usually looks. Similarly, Kafka's father (who specialises in work on the subconscious) is killed potentially by Kafka, even though we know that what is actually happening is Nakata killing Johnnie Walker. The surrealism in the events follows the logic of dreams, but the characters all accept with a nod that things are happening as they are.

Murakami implies that within Japan, reality is questionable: "God's always been kind of a flexible concept [...] If you think God's there, He is. If you don't, He isn't" (p. 308). Although he suggests that this is true "especially in Japan" (*ibid.*), the reader learns over the course of the novel to think of each passing event as a riddle without an answer. As if teaching a new way of thinking about literature and narrative logic, *Kafka on the Shore* invites numerous interpretations, and just like the way the characters interpret the events going on around them, the strange and macabre are not necessarily incorrect. As readers, Murakami's novel asks us to read a little differently, to suspend our disbelief about reality in order to arrive at a place in which the rest of the novel's themes can come together coherently.

FATE

Fate is one of the main driving forces in the novel for most of the characters. The prophesy given to him by his father pushes Kafka towards Oshima and Miss Saeki, and pushes him towards fulfilling his Oedipal curse. Miss Saeki feels that her fate was sealed when her boyfriend died decades before, and refuses to go on living because of it. She believes her fate is to suffer. And Nakata, whether he realises it or not, plays a role driven by fate, meeting Hoshino and carrying out task after task because he believes he ought to, and because of an accident that befell *him* on a fateful day. While in the grip of this powerful, unseen force, each of the characters finds themselves pushed into ever more danger or unhappiness.

Kafka refuses to believe the truth about himself, preferring instead to rely on fate to make his decisions for him: "Strong and independent? I'm neither. I'm just being pushed along by reality, whether I like it or not" (p. 268). This false belief that he is not an agent of free will, and that reality, although certainly flexible, is unwavering in its plans for him, leads him to a point in his life of great internal struggle. Although Miss Saeki refuses to tell Kafka that she is his mother, and provides good evidence to the contrary, Kafka believes it wholeheartedly, as he does with Sakura, who is not his sister but just a close friend he met randomly on a bus. The thing that most stifles Kafka is his inability to believe in accidents despite their prominence in his life and the lives of those he cares for.

Ultimately, Hoshino provides the novel with what may well be Murakami's overriding message on fate. Despite the things that have got him down and the fact he was living a life without anything interesting happening to him, he believes in the promise of the future:

> "Still, you know, interesting things do happen in life – like with us now. I'm not sure why. My grandpa used to say that things never work out like you think they will, but that's what makes life interesting, and that makes sense." (p. 329)

Hoshino starts to believe that the things that have happened to him in the past do not have to dictate what happens to him in the future. He suggests that life is an interesting ride when you let things happen to you that you are not expecting. Unlike Kafka, who seems to see every event that befalls him as some part of a prophesy, or something endowed with great meaning, Hoshino recognises that sometimes things just happen. Just like reality, fate is something that is changing and cannot be understood in a logical way.

FURTHER REFLECTION

SOME QUESTIONS TO THINK ABOUT...

- Do you think that Miss Saeki was Kafka's mother? Explain your answer.
- Why do you think Murakami used commercial brands like KFC and Johnnie Walker in creating some of his characters?
- Why do you think both Nakata and Miss Saeki die after meeting one another?
- Where/what do you think the cabin that Kafka gets taken to by the soldiers is?
- Why does Murakami let Nakata, and later Hoshino, speak to cats?
- Do you think the open-ended riddles employed by Murakami's narrative are an effective way of creating meaning, or do they make it more difficult?
- Why does Kafka go back to Tokyo at the end rather than stay where he is?
- Why do you think Murakami had his character choose the name 'Kafka'?

*We want to hear from you!
Leave a comment on your online library
and share your favourite books on social media!*

FURTHER READING

REFERENCE EDITION

- Murakami, H. (2005) *Kafka on the Shore*. London: Vintage.

REFERENCE STUDIES

- Meads, J. (2018) Into the Labyrinth: the Dream Logic of Kafka on the Shore. *Steppenwolf*. [Online]. [Accessed 15 February 2019]. Available from: <https://www.steppenwolf.org/articles/into-the-labyrinth-the-dream-logic-of-kafka-on-the-shore/>

MORE FROM BRIGHTSUMMARIES.COM

- Reading guide – *Norwegian Wood* by Haruki Murakami.

Bright ≡Summaries.com

More guides to rediscover your love of literature

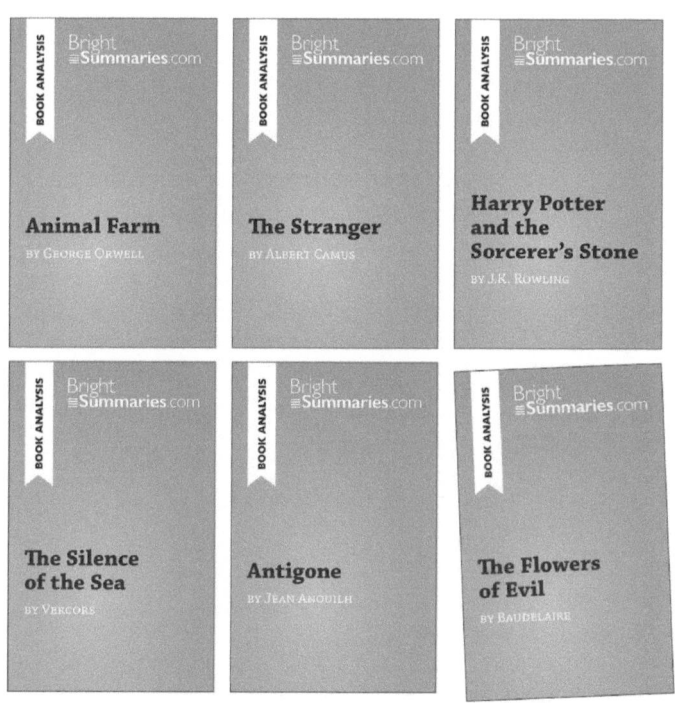

www.brightsummaries.com

Although the editor makes every effort to verify the accuracy of the information published, BrightSummaries.com accepts no responsibility for the content of this book.

© BrightSummaries.com, 2019. All rights reserved.

www.brightsummaries.com

Ebook EAN: 9782808018630

Paperback EAN: 9782808018647

Legal Deposit: D/2019/12603/98

Cover: © Primento

Digital conception by Primento, the digital partner of publishers.